To everyone who's wondered if there's someone like them. —A. B. & L. E.

Library of Congress Cataloging-in-Publication Data available.

ISBN 978-1-4521-6337-6

Manufactured in China.

Design by Leo Espinosa and Sara Gillingham Studio.
Typeset in Futura Demi.
Hand-lettering by Leo Espinosa.
The illustrations in this book were rendered in Adobe Photoshop.

10 9 8 7 6 5 4 3 2 1

Chronicle Books LLC
680 Second Street, San Francisco, California 94107
www.chroniclekids.com

Written by
New York Times–bestselling author
Annie Barrows

Illustrated by
Pura Belpré honoree
Leo Espinosa

chronicle books·san francisco

Hello.

You are you, and I am I. We are people. Also known as humans. This makes us different from most of the things on Earth.

We are not at all like tin cans.
We are not shaped like tin cans.
We cannot hold tomato sauce like tin cans.

If you open up our lids, nothing good happens.

We are not at all
like tin cans.

What about a swimming pool?

We are a little bit more like a swimming pool than a tin can. Like a swimming pool, we have water and chemicals and dirt inside us.

But unlike a swimming pool, we don't have people splashing around inside us.

Also, we have feet.
We can run away into
the trees if we want to.
Poor swimming pool.

We are a little bit
like a swimming pool.

Here is a mushroom.

Wow! We are way more like a mushroom
than a swimming pool!

Mushrooms grow, like we do. They need air and water and food, like we do. They make more mushrooms, like we do (okay, okay, we don't make mushrooms; we make people).

But mushrooms don't have anything to say, and even if they did, they wouldn't have a way to say it. They don't have mouths. They don't have brains either.

It's not a rude thing to say. It's the truth.

We are like a mushroom in a few ways,
but we are more different than we are alike.

Look at this thing!

This is an excavator!

It digs up big piles of dirt and moves them around. We can do that too, but we can't do it nearly as well as an excavator.

Is an excavator better than we are?

Let's see.

Can an excavator tell a joke?
No!

Can an excavator fry an egg?
No!

Can an excavator burp?

Absolutely not!
It's got no brain, no mouth, no ideas.

An excavator can do two
things better than we can.
But we can do many, many
more things than an excavator.

Burp!

This is a hyena.

We are more like a hyena
than we are like a tin can,
a swimming pool,
a mushroom,
or an excavator.

Hyenas and humans (that's us!)
need food, air, and water to live.
Neither humans nor hyenas are
made in a factory, like tin cans.

Neither of us grows out of the ground, like mushrooms.

Nope, we have little baby humans

Hyenas have brains, like we do.
They run around really fast, like we do.
They make loud noises, like we do.

But hyenas don't say words. They don't tell stories.
They don't get embarrassed, even when they're caught
eating something off the ground.

They don't know when their birthday is,
and if you invited a hyena over to your
house next Thursday, it wouldn't come.
Hyenas don't make plans.

Which is fine, because if a hyena
did come to your house, it might
try to eat your baby brother.

So we are like hyenas in some ways,
but if you were a hyena,
you wouldn't be like you are now.
And I would run away if I saw you.

Hey! It's me! And there's you!
Look at us!
Are we alike?

We are not exactly alike.

But we are both humans,
so we have to eat food and
breathe air and drink water.

We both have to sleep.
We both wear clothes
(most of the time).

We both have brains that let us
tell stories and burp and joke.

We know when our birthdays are.
Sometimes we get embarrassed.

We are SO MUCH alike!

Even if you get embarrassed when you fall out of your chair, and I get embarrassed when the teacher calls on me, you are more like me than you are like an excavator.

Even if I eat raspberry Jell-O with bananas in it,
and you would never ever eat that in a million years,
I am more like you than a mushroom.

Even if you speak a language I don't speak,
you are more like me than a hyena.

See that guy?

He's more like us than he's
like a swimming pool.

So is she.

Even that really old lady
over there—she's like us too
(but more wrinkled).

Wait. Look at all these people.

They are not exactly like us.
But they are more like us
than they are different.

I am more like you than I am
like most of the things on Earth.

I'm glad.

I'd rather be like you than like a mushroom.